Grimm's Fairy Tales

For Lily Galea Pirotta
S.P.

For my mum
C.J.

ORCHARD BOOKS
338 Euston Road, London NW1 3BH
Orchard Books Australia
Level 17/207 Kent Street, Sydney, NSW 2000

This text was first published in the form of a gift collection called
The Sleeping Princess by Orchard Books in 2002

This edition first published in hardback in 2012
First paperback publication in 2013

ISBN 978 1 40830 833 2 (hardback)
ISBN 978 1 40830 834 9 (paperback)

A CIP catalogue record for this book is available
from the British Library.

1 3 5 7 9 10 8 6 4 2 (hardback)
1 3 5 7 9 10 8 6 4 2 (paperback)

Printed in China

Orchard Books is a division of Hachette Children's Books,
an Hachette UK company.
www.hachette.co.uk

Grimm's Fairy Tales

Snow White and Rose Red

Written by Saviour Pirotta

Illustrated by Cecilia Johansson

ORCHARD

A poor woman had two rose trees growing outside her cottage, one with beautiful white flowers and the other with red. She also had twin girls, named after the rose trees. Rose Red and Snow White!

Every night the two girls would sit and listen to their mother reading a fairy tale. One winter's evening, just as they were finishing their story, there was a loud knock on the door.

Rose Red opened it, and an enormous brown bear stuck his snout inside.

The two girls jumped back, afraid.

"I mean you no harm," the bear said. "I just want to warm my paws by the fire."

So the bear was allowed to come in and sit down. The girls' mother went on with the story and bit by bit the girls came closer to the bear and leaned against his warm fur for comfort.

In the morning, the girls let the bear out
and he wandered off in the snow.

But that evening he
returned to hear more stories.

And he kept coming back till the spring.

Then, one day, the bear said, "I shall not return tonight. I must go to the mountains to guard my treasure from the dwarves.

"In winter, when the ground is frozen, they cannot dig my gold up, but in spring when the ground is soft, they steal it."

Snow White and Rose Red were sad,
for they had grown very fond of the bear.
Snow White opened the door, and the
bear was soon lost to sight.

Not long afterwards, Snow White and Rose Red went to the forest to collect firewood. On their way back they came across a dwarf jumping up and down like a grasshopper. His long beard was trapped under a fallen tree trunk.

The girls pulled on the beard to set him free, but it was no use. So Snow White whipped out a pair of scissors and – *snip, snip* – she cut off the ends.

"How can I go about with the tip of my beard missing, you silly, insolent creatures?" roared the dwarf. "It's a good job it will grow back quickly."

And without so much as a thank you, he
pulled a bag of gold out of the hollow tree
trunk and disappeared into the forest with it.

The girls hoped they would never run into the ungrateful dwarf again but only a week later they met him once more by a brook. As they approached the water, they saw the rude dwarf leaping about.

"My beard has got tangled in the fishing line," snapped the dwarf. "And a big fish is about to pull me into the water. Don't just stand there watching me drown!"

The girls tried very hard to free the dwarf from the line but it was no use. So, once again, Snow White produced her sewing scissors and – *snip, snip* – she cut off a good portion of the dwarf's beard.

"Are you mad?" howled the dwarf, the moment he was free. "You have ruined my face completely!" And with that, he fished a bag of pearls out from among the reeds and disappeared down the road.

A week later, the girls were on their way to the market when they saw an eagle wheeling overhead.

The large bird
landed behind a big
rock and a moment
later the girls heard
someone howling.
The eagle had snatched up
their old friend the dwarf
by his trousers!

21

"Get over here and help me!" cried the dwarf. "Can't you see this monster is about to have me for its breakfast?"

At once, the girls grabbed the dwarf by the coat-tails and started pulling. They pulled and pulled until they had tugged the dwarf right out of the eagle's claws.

"You clumsy creatures," said the dwarf.
"My coat is torn to shreds!"
Then he prised a bag of
diamonds out from under
the rock and was gone.

On their way home from the market, the girls bumped into the dwarf a fourth time. He was sitting on the grass with his diamonds scattered around him.

"What are you gawping at?" shouted the dwarf. "Have you never seen diamonds before? Be off with you, you thieves—"

He was still raging when a bear leaped
out of the trees and pounced on him.
The bear raised his enormous paw
and – *thwack* – he gave the dwarf
a mighty blow and sent him flying.

The girls screamed and started running.
But the bear called after them, "Snow White,
Rose Red, wait for me."

The girls recognised their old friend and stopped. As the bear caught up with them, his claws disappeared, his fur melted away and there stood a handsome prince.

"I am the king's son," he said. "That wicked dwarf stole my treasure and put a spell on me, to live as a bear until the dwarf was punished. Now I am free to go home."

Soon Snow White married the prince and
Rose Red married his twin brother.

The girls' mother came to live with them in the palace and she brought her two rose trees with her. Every year they continued to bear the most beautiful blooms: snow white and rose red.